visit us at www.abdopublishing.com

Reinforced library bound edition published in 2012 by Spotlight, a division of the ABDO Group, 8000 West 78th Street, Edina, Minnesota 55439. Spotlight produces high-quality reinforced library bound editions for schools and libraries. Published by agreement with Warner Bros.—A Time Warner Company. The stories, characters, and incidents mentioned are entirely fictional. All rights reserved. Used under authorization.

Printed in the United States of America, Melrose Park, Illinois.
052011
092011
 This book contains at least 10% recycled materials.

Library of Congress Cataloging-in-Publication Data

Griep, Terrance.
  Scooby-Doo in Chills and spills! / writer, Terrance Griep ;
penciller, Leo Batic. -- Reinforced library bound ed.
    p. cm. -- (Scooby-Doo graphic novels)
  ISBN 978-1-59961-919-4
1. Graphic novels. I. Scooby-Doo (Television program) II. Title.
III. Title: Chills and spills!
PZ7.7.G75Sb 2011
741.5'973--dc22
                        2011001367

All Spotlight books are reinforced library bindings
and manufactured in the United States of America.

SCOOBY-DOO!

Table of Contents

I REALLY APPRECIATE THIS, *FRED*. IF I'M GOING TO WIN THE WAKEBOARDING CHAMPIONSHIP ULTRA-TOUR, I'LL NEED EVERY BIT OF PRACTICE I CAN GET.

ARE YOU KIDDING? YOU'RE *TAD LAURENT! THE* TAD LAURENT! YOU'RE THE TOP-RATED WAKEBOARDER IN THE SOLAR SYSTEM-- WE'RE HAPPY TO HELP...

I KNOW THAT WE'RE HERE TO COMPETE, *VELMA*, BUT IT ALMOST SEEMS LIKE A WASTE--THIS PLACE SEEMS SO PEACEFUL...

MAYBE THAT'S WHY THE LOCALS NAMED IT DREAM LAKE, *DAPHNE*.

I DIDN'T WANT TO THREATEN MY REP AS A HEPSTER, SO I DIDN'T, LIKE, ASK TAD, BUT...

...JUST WHAT *IS* WAKEBOARDING ANYWAY?

REAH!

WELL, *SHAGGY, SCOOBY*, THE WAVE CREATED BEHIND A SPEED BOAT IS CALLED ITS WAKE. THE WAKEBOARDER USES THAT WAVE TO PERFORM STUNTS...

READY, FREDDIE!

SLEEPER'S PEEPERS

TERRANCE GRIEP -- WRITER   LEO BATIC -- PENCILLER   HORACIO OTTOLINI -- INKER
TRAVIS LANHAM -- LETTERER   HEROIC AGE -- COLORIST   VINCENT DEPORTER -- COVER   HARVEY RICHARDS -- EDITOR

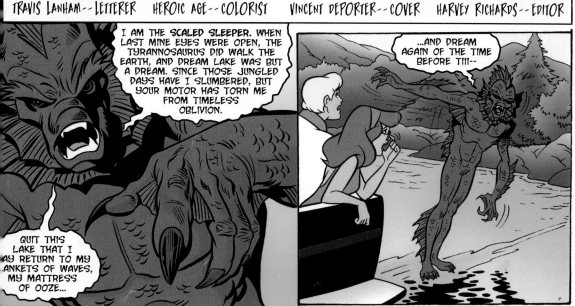

WELL, CHNICALLY, S A *LAKE* ONSTER... UT YES.

IT'S THE *MONSTER* PART I HAVE A PROBLEM WITH, OKAY? ALL I CARE ABOUT IS THAT THE TOURNAMENT IS ALLOWED TO HAPPEN.

CALL ME A POSER, NATHAN, BUT I DON'T THINK I WANT TO GET INTO A LAKE THAT'S HOME TURF TO A MONSTER, LAKE, SEA, OR OTHERWISE.

LOOK WHO IT IS--*MICKEY "RED RIBBON" BRODY.* MAYBE YOU JUST DON'T WANT TO GET IN A LAKE WHERE TAD LAURENT IS COMPETING--HASN'T HE BEATEN YOU EVERY TIME THE TWO OF YOU HAVE BOARDED?

W-WELL, YEAH... BUT I'M SURE I COULD WIN THIS TIME...AFTER PLYING MY NEW MOVE-SET.

ARE YOU SUGGESTING THAT I'M SOMEHOW BEHIND THIS MONSTER, MR. DAY? MAYBE YOU ARE--MAYBE YOU CAN'T STAND THE THOUGHT OF DECLARING ME THE WINNER OF YOUR TOUR!

WAWAOOHH!

WOULDN'T *THAT* BE A TRIP?

OO. FACEPLANT.

OWPHPHPH!

...WE'RE GOING TO HAVE TO LURE THE SCALED SLEEPER TO US.

OKAY, FRED, OKAY-- I WAS WILLING TO HUMOR YOUR RUMOR, BEING AS EVERY OTHER WAKEBOARD-WORTHY PERSON IS, LIKE, SNOOZING, I WAS WILLING TO GEAR UP AND COME OUT ON THE LAKE IN THE MIDDLE OF THE NIGHT.

I WAS WILLING TO PLAY ALONG UP TO THIS POINT... BUT I WON'T MAKE WITH THE WAVES AS MONSTER BAIT, NO MATTER WHAT YOUR CRAZY PLAN FOR A MONSTER TRAP IS.

Y'DIG THAT, BOSSCAT? NOTHING, AND I MEAN, *NOTHING* WILL GET ME INTO THAT WATER...

NOTHING, SHAGGY? NOT EVEN... *THAT?*

YOU ARE ONE SNEAKY, SNEAKY SQUARE, FRED JONES.

NOW, SHRILL ONE, SHALL YOU HEAR THE SOUND OF MY--

FLUMP

K-HFLUMP

HYOLP!

OBOY.

UT--I GUESS THIS MEANS I MAKE GROOVY MONSTER BAIT!

AH, WELL...

"...AT LEAST THINGS CAN'T GET ANY SCREWIER!"

FREDDIE, LOOK--THAT RAMP. MAYBE WE CAN--

GOOD EYE, VELMA. IT'S SO DARK OUT HERE...

HERE! WE! GO!

RAHRHRH

SHRP SHRP SHRP SNAP

SCOOBY! SHAGGY!

JUMPING HEELSIDES! DOESN'T ANYONE *SLEEP* AROUND THESE PARTS? WHAT'S ALL THE RACKET?

I WAS WORKING ON MY NEW MOVE-SET WHEN I HEARD ALL THE SHOUTING. AND THE YELLING. AND THE MOTORING. AND THE CRASHING. AND THE SHOUTING. AND THE YELLING.

WHAT'S...?

...GOING ON? NOT MUCH--WE'RE SOLVING THE MYSTERY, IS ALL. WHICH BRINGS US TO OUR SLUMBEROUS FRIEND HERE...

WELL, IF EVERYONE ELSE IS ACCOUNTED FOR, THEN THE SCALED SLEEPER MUST BE...

HARMON PALUMBO!

THE END